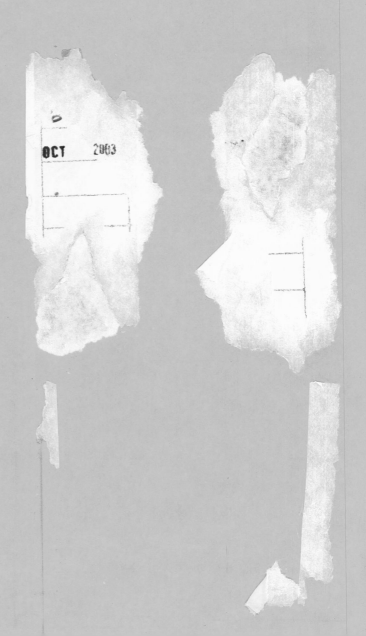

FRANZ BRANDENBERG

What's Wrong with a Van?

Pictures by A L I K I

Greenwillow Books, New York

Printed in Hong Kong by South China Printing Co.
First Edition   10 9 8 7 6 5 4 3 2 1

Colored pencils and watercolor paints
were combined with a black line for
the full-color art.
The text type is Souvenir.

Library of Congress Cataloging-in-Publication Data
Brandenberg, Franz.
What's wrong with a van?
Summary: Edward and Elizabeth think they want
a new family car that is not dented or in need
of paint, until the beloved old van is taken
away and they find themselves missing it.
[1. Vans—Fiction]   I. Aliki, ill.   II. Title.
PZ7.B7364Whc 1987   [E]   86-9842
ISBN 0-688-06773-5
ISBN 0-688-06775-1 (lib. bdg.)

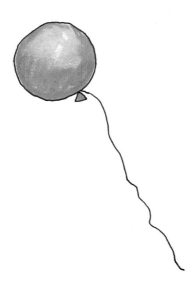

For Jason and Alexa
and all the rest
of the passengers

"Our neighbors got a nice new car," said
Edward.

"As a surprise," said Elizabeth.

"When will we get a new car?" asked Edward.

"We don't need a new car," said Father.

"Our old one is still good enough."

"But the paint is peeling," said Edward.
"And the hubcaps are rusty and the
bumpers are dented."
"And the seat covers are worn," said
Elizabeth.

"The truth is," said Mother, "the exhaust backfires and the engine makes a funny noise."

"And worst of all, it's not even a car—it's a van," said Elizabeth.

"Everyone else has a car," said Edward.

"Why can't we have one?" asked Elizabeth.

"We'll see," said Father.

"All those nice memories," said Mother
when Father drove the old van away.
"We had so much fun with it," said
Elizabeth.

"We are going to miss it," said Edward.

"We played in it, we ate in it, we sometimes
even slept in it," said Elizabeth.

"We did everything except have parties in it."

"We took great trips in it," said Edward.
"We visited our grandparents, aunts,
uncles, and cousins in it. We drove to
the shore and the mountains in it."

"Oh, I left my bamboo stick under the seat," said Elizabeth.

"And I forgot my rock crystal in the ashtray," said Edward.

"It's too late now," said Elizabeth.

"I hope the new car will be as nice as the old van," said Edward.
"You'll be surprised," said Father.

"Another van!" said Elizabeth. "It looks
  just like the old one."
"But the paint is all shiny, the hubcaps
  aren't rusty, and the bumpers aren't
  dented," said Edward.

"The seat covers aren't worn," said
  Elizabeth.
"The engine doesn't make funny noises
  and the exhaust doesn't backfire,"
  said Mother.
"I'm glad it's a van and not just a car,"
  said Elizabeth.

"Look, my bamboo stick is under the seat!" said Elizabeth.

"And my rock crystal is in the ashtray!" said Edward. "Just like in the old van."

"It is the old van," said Father. "I just
   had it overhauled."
"What a surprise!" said Elizabeth.
"Welcome back, old van!" said Edward.
"We missed you!" said Mother.

"We'll take more great trips in it,"
said Edward.

"We'll play in it, eat in it, and sleep in it,"
said Elizabeth.

"And we'll have a party in it right now," said Mother.

"We could never have done this
   in an ordinary car," said Edward.
"There is nothing like a van!"
   said Elizabeth.
"Long live the new old van!"
   they toasted.